Weekly Reader Books presents

An Early I Can Read Book

Will You Cross Me?

by Marilyn Kaye

Pictures by

Ned Delaney

Harper & Row, Publishers

This book is a presentation of Weekly Reader Books.
Weekly Reader Books offers book clubs for children from
preschool through high school.

For further information write to:
Weekly Reader Books
4343 Equity Drive
Columbus, Ohio 43228

WILL YOU CROSS ME?
Text copyright © 1985 by Marilyn Kaye
Illustrations copyright © 1985 by T. N. Delaney III
All rights reserved. No part of this book may be
used or reproduced in any manner whatsoever without
written permission except in the case of brief quotations
embodied in critical articles and reviews. Printed in
the United States of America. For information address
Harper & Row Junior Books, 10 East 53rd Street,
New York, N.Y. 10022. Published simultaneously in
Canada by Fitzhenry & Whiteside Limited, Toronto.

Library of Congress Cataloging in Publication Data
Kaye, Marilyn
   Will you cross me?

   (An Early I can read book)
   Summary: Two friends living on opposite sides of the
street must rely on passersby to help them cross the
street to play with each other.
   [1. Friendship—Fiction. 2. Play—Fiction]
I. Delaney, T. N. III, ill.   II. Title.   III. Series.
PZ7.K2127Wi 1985   [E]   84-47633
ISBN 0-06-023102-5
ISBN 0-06-023103-3 (lib. bdg.)

            1 2 3 4 5 6 7 8 9 10
                    First Edition

*I Can Read Book is a registered trademark of Harper & Row,
Publishers, Inc.*

For all the kids on Tenth Street,
Park Slope, Brooklyn,
and especially
Barry and Neal
—M.K.

For Terry Vonnegut
—N.D.

"Hey, Joe!

Want to play ball?"

called Sam.

"Sure!

Come on over!"

Joe yelled.

Sam ran up to a big boy

walking down the street.

"Will you cross me?" Sam asked.

The boy did not hear him.

Sam called to Joe,

"You come over here."

Joe saw a woman

running up the street.

"Will you cross me?" he asked.

"Can't stop!" she said, and ran on.

"Will you cross me?"

Sam asked a girl with red shoes.

"Sure!" said the girl.

"Will you cross me?"

Joe asked the man with a green hat.

"Come along," said the man.

11

"Oh, no!" cried Sam.

"Now what are we going to do?"

"Throw me the ball," yelled Joe.

"I can pitch it to you."

"Here goes!" called Sam.

A lady with a bag

came out of her house.

"You kids stop that!" she said.

"That is not safe."

"Then will you cross me?" asked Joe.

The lady took Joe across the street.

"Now we can really play," said Sam.

"Give me the ball.

I want to pitch."

"No, I want to pitch," Joe said.

"It is my ball!" said Sam.

"But you threw it to me!"

Joe yelled.

"Now I want it back!" Sam cried.

"No fair!" hollered Joe.

"It is my ball,

and I get to choose," Sam yelled.

"You can have the bat."

Joe threw the ball down.

"No!" Joe said.

"Take your old ball and go home!"

"Will you cross me?"

Sam asked the man with the dog.

"All right," said the man.

"Hey, Joe," called Sam.

"You can pitch."

"Okay, come on over,"

Joe called back.

"Will you cross me?"

Sam asked the lady with the baby.

"Of course," said the lady.

24

"*Now* we can play ball," said Sam.

"Here goes the pitch!" called Joe.

Joe's mother looked out the window.

"Joe, come in the house," she called.

"Do I have to?" asked Joe.

"Yes," she said, "right now."

Joe gave the ball back to Sam.

"Too bad," he said.

"Yeah," said Sam.

"Let's play again tomorrow."

28

"Okay," said Joe,

"see you tomorrow."

"Will you cross me?"

"Will you cross me?"

"Hey, somebody!

Anybody!

WILL YOU CROSS ME?"